BEIPIAOSAURUS

PACHYRHINOSAURUS

SAUROPELTA

AFROVENATOR

SCAPHOGNATHUS

BARAPASAURUS

SAUROLOPHUS

ALBERTOSAURUS

LYSTROSAURUS

THECODONT

P9-CSV-759

JANE YOLEN

How Do Dinosaurs Say

I'M MAD?

Illustrated by

MARK TEAGUE

THE BLUE SKY PRESS
An Imprint of Scholastic Inc. · New York

Everybody gets angry sometimes. Kids do. So do parents. Sometimes we get angry when we're scared, or want something we can't have, or are feeling mean or feeling sick. Anger can be very frightening, and it can make people sad. But there are lots of ways to learn how to control anger, just as the dinosaurs do in this book. Some of them count to ten, some of them have a time out, and some of them take deep breaths. Then, when the dinosaurs are calm again, they clean up any mess they've made, they say, "I'm sorry," and they give big hugs. Just as you do.

THE BLUE SKY PRESS

Text copyright © 2013 by Jane Yolen · Illustrations copyright © 2013 by Mark Teague

All rights reserved. No part of this publication may be reproduced, stored in a retrieval system, or transmitted in any form or by any means, electronic, mechanical, photocopying, recording, or otherwise, without written permission of the publisher. For information regarding permission, please write to: Permissions Department, Scholastic Inc., 557 Broadway, New York, New York 10012.

SCHOLASTIC, THE BLUE SKY PRESS, and associated logos are trademarks and/or registered trademarks of Scholastic Inc.

Library of Congress card catalog number: 2012040941

ISBN 978-0-545-14315-8

10 9 8 7 6 5 4 3 2 1   13 14 15 16 17

Printed in Malaysia   108

First printing, October 2013

Designed by Kathleen Westray

For Zoe and Lucy Krosoczka,
too cute to be mad
dinosaurs
J. Y.

For Butch
M. T.

How does a dinosaur act

when he's mad?

BARAPASAURUS

Does he roar,

slam the door,

yell at Mom

or at Dad?

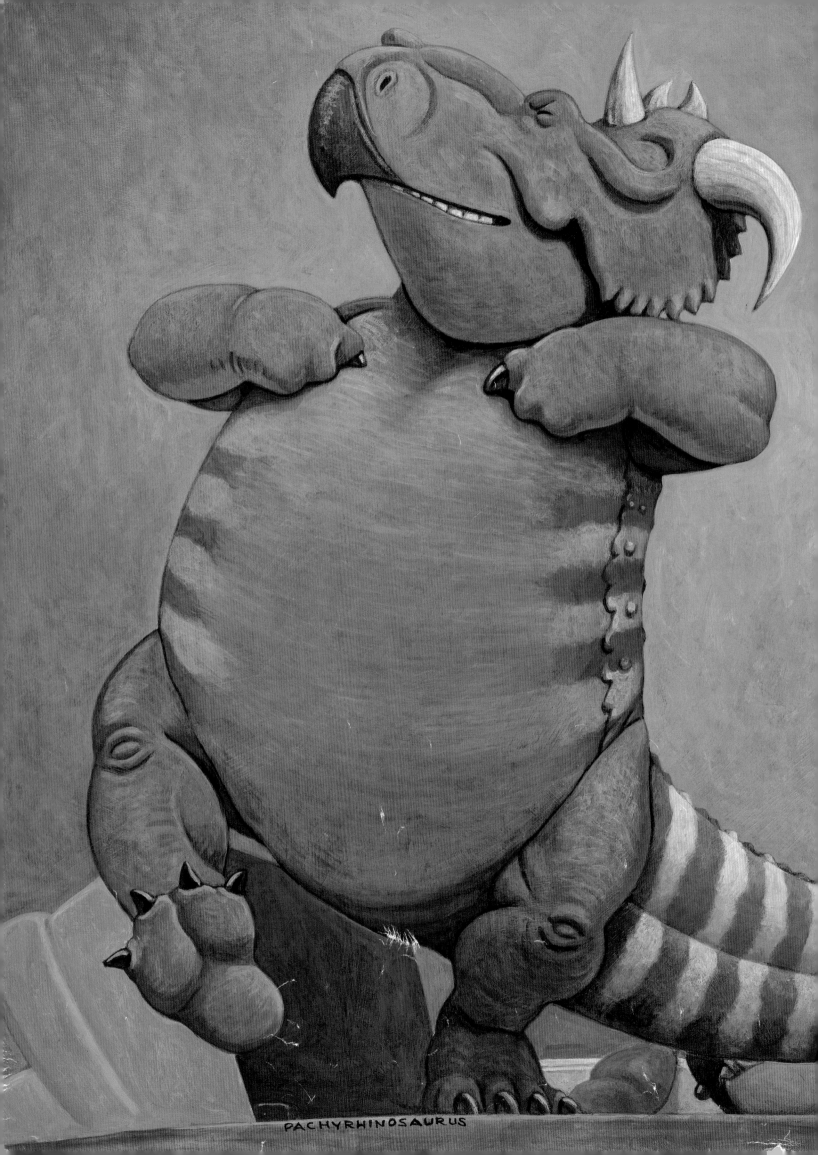

PACHYRHINOSAURUS

When he can't get his way,
does he boast, "I'll be bad!"
Is that what dinosaurs say
when they're mad?

When Papa says, "No!"
does he grumble
and pout?

When Mama says, "No!"

does he throw

toys about?

THECODONT

When he's told
to sit still,
does he kick
at a chair?

Does he act as if
Mother and Father
aren't there?

When he hears, "Take a nap!"
does he give dirty looks?
When he's told, "Quiet down!"
does he rip up his books?

No cookies today?

Fling a mug

at the cat!

"Time for bed!"

Does he bang on the floor

with his bat?

No . . .

a dinosaur

doesn't—

he counts up to ten,

then after a time out,

breathes calmly . . .

and then . . .

he cleans up his mess,
and he picks up
the mug.

He says,
"I'm so sorry."
He gives
a big hug.

His anger is gone,

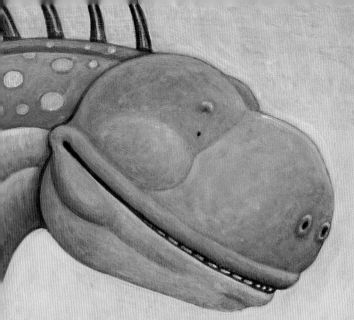

so he opens the door.

Not mad? I'm so glad,

little dinosaur.

BEIPIAOSAURUS

PACHYRHINOSAURUS

SAUROPELTA

AFROVENATOR

SCAPHOGNATHUS

BARAPASAURUS

SAUROLOPHUS

ALBERTOSAURUS

LYSTROSAURUS

THECODONT